Sweet Temptation

By

M. S. Spencer

Copyright © 2023 by - M. S. Spencer - All Rights Reserved.

It is not legal to reproduce, duplicate, or transmit any part of this document in either electronic means or printed format. Recording of this publication is strictly prohibited.

Dedication

This book wouldn't have been possible without the help of the following people:

My family who stands by me through thick and thin.

Nath, toujours utiliser les cinq sens n'est-ce pas? Pour ta relecture et tes bons mots! Merci pour les remue-méninges, les débats d'idées et ta précieuse amitié.

Gizzy, thank you for the proofreading, the sarcasm, and the memes.

Nads, thank you for your friendship and for believing in me.

Sam, the muse, the inspiration. Who would've thought that by following you on social media, we would become friends? Thank you for the help and the investment, you have no idea how much I appreciate it.

Love you guys xx

Table of Contents

Dedication ii
Chapter 1 1
Chapter 2 8
Chapter 3 27
Chapter 4 36
Chapter 5 46
About the Author 66

Chapter 1

Dalton

"Ah! Fucking hell!"

My head's pounding. The digits on the clock, blur as weird red goblin eyes glowing in the dark, indicate that somehow, I made it back alive last night, and it's way past Noon. Seems I've been partying quite hard. I stretch and sigh, wasted, yes, not totally shitfaced, though. Some glass tinkling from the kitchen gets my attention. *Am I not alone?* I'm not sure, I believe Miles told me something about his little sis coming over for Spring break.

Been ages since I've seen her.

I smile to myself, remembering that the girl used to have a huge crush on me. Teenage wet dreams kinda shit.

You were a horny kid yourself back then, mate, and if you're honest with yourself, you still are.

Getting my sorry self out of bed, I grab a pair of grey sweatpants lying around and put them on before walking to the restroom. I glance up at my reflection.

Not too bad for a bloke who got in completely hammered at 3 a.m.

Running a hand through my long messy hair, I look at my undercut to see if it needs shaving. Splashing water over my face, I think back to when I used to go up to Miles' house. Even though I admit, now, I was interested in her, Sophie was off limits. Because, well, we don't fuck best mates' little sisters, do we? But she's always been a cutie, I smirk, wondering what she will look like now that she is all grown up. According to big bro, she's single and ready to mingle, enjoying what life has to offer, no strings attached.

My kind of lady.

With headphones on my ears, I navigate to the living room.

Well, well, look what the cat dragged in.

Sitting with her legs tucked under her, laying back in an armchair, Sophie's reading. I try my best to weave my ass to the kitchen, not to disturb her, but also because I'd love to keep my morning routine going on. Music, coffee, and no small talk for now. The book must be particularly fascinating because she doesn't even bat an eye as I enter the room. She's really just as I remember her, but older. Plump. Sexier.

I grin and dampen my lower lip before swallowing a sip of coffee, still gazing at her.

I can't help but wonder if this crush is still living somewhere.

Her curvy legs wrapped in black jeans start fluttering, but I don't believe I'm the cause of it. What kind of novel would make a girl squeeze her thighs together like that? The answer coming to mind has me grinning. The way she bites her lips while concentrating is absolutely fucking adorable. Under her teeth, the flesh bursts out, pink, luscious, and sensual. This mouth would probably do wonders on my body. Unaware of my presence, she's completely absorbed in her book. Her red hair dances and falls slowly over her bare shoulders, peeking out of her loose grey top.

Why do I want to tug at it?

Smirking, I let my eyes travel over her body as I imagine all the fun ways we could celebrate our reunion.

Fuck, mate, calm down!

Little sisters are off-limits, remember?

Even though she isn't so little anymore.

I run my fingertips up and down my arm, distracted, tracing the lines of my most recent tattoo. The demon face inked into my skin stares back at me, one beast winking at the other.

How do I come up with something clever to say now?

Zoning out a bit, I dive into the music, wondering how to start the conversation. I stretch out my arms, cracking my neck. Under my lashes, I catch a glimpse of reaction. A not-so-shy first look from behind her book and blushing cheeks.

There you go, Princess.

I watch her incredulous eyes lingering over my body, inevitably ogling, squinting even, lower and lower, along my obliques and further down to my crotch.

How do you picture it, Princess? How would you like it to be? Bet you read plenty of juicy details in your steamy novels.

I squeeze my eyes shut, picturing the typical scenario in those kinds of books.

When does the bad boy push the nice girl against the wall? Cause there are plenty of walls here, and I'm as bad as they come.

Christ! Lucky for me, she can't read minds.

I slowly open my eyes and lock them on to hers while weaving around the room. Relaxed, sly, and ready to play, I grin at her. Sophie seems troubled; her confusion adds to my own pleasure. I bite my lower lip, amused. You could say I'm an ass, and you'd probably be right, but this is way too easy to pass up.

Keep it up, Princess, since you seem to be enjoying what you're seeing so much.

I wonder how her brother would react seeing me tease his little sister like that. He might just kill me, protective as he is of Sophie. He probably doesn't even know she once sent me quite the love letter. A very passionate one at that.

Does she remember?

"How long have you been here?" she asks shyly.

I move the headphones on my neck as Falling in Reverse is blasting away.

"I live here, Princess."

Seeing the surprise on her face, I laugh and shake my head.

"What's with the face? You didn't imagine I'd avoid you all week, did you?"

She brushes off my question.

"You've got quite a versatile taste," she mocks, pointing at my headphones.

"What, am I supposed to only listen to hard-core music?" I ask with a coy smile. "That's rude!"

Her grey irises are holding my gaze as she nods.

"Yeah, I guess I judged you a little too fast there, haven't I?"

"For future reference, your Highness," I reply with a sarcastic tone. "I also like good ol' rock'n'roll as well as a little bit of pop punk music."

"I apologize Dalton. I forgot you're a man full of surprises."

"Oh, you have no idea, Princess."

I smile broadly, ferociously, as I come closer to her, delighted by the sound of my name in her mouth and the citrusy fragrance of her hair coming up as I lean forward. As I stand above her, Sophie shudders, her soft skin almost brushing mine. A gentle warmth radiates from her body despite the goosebumps running up her arms. Her pupils widen like a deer caught in headlights as I stand there, my upside-down cross necklace oscillating in the void left between us. I tilt my head, pretending a sudden interest in the book she's now clutching to. Doing so, I feel my hair fall off over my shoulders, tickling her face, creating a wall hiding us from the outside world. I swear I hear her insult me mentally. Her breathing lightly speeds up while my eyes roam over her perfect features.

Annoyed? Excited? Can't tell yet.

"You okay there, Soph?" I ask, my voice a bit strained.

Holding my gaze, she furiously blushes as if she couldn't be any cuter.

She gently hooks the silver chain with her slender finger, pulling me closer. I notice she must have recently got her nails done. Sharp and painted black, I wonder what they'd feel like digging into my back. This game is driving me mad, and I am very tempted to forget whatever bullshit I promised not to do to her.

What does she taste like?

Sea salt and sugar. Rain and clementines.

Lust and forbidden fruit.

I deeply breathe in and close my eyes for a second. I have got to get my composure back. I open them again and scrutinize her face. Her grey irises sparkle, mischievous. She arches an eyebrow, a provocative fingertip brushing her full, inviting lips. She's a clever little minx this one. My eyes follow the lines of her heart-shaped face; her small doll-like nose is just a little snub, gold freckles scattered on her blushing cheeks, and a little scar indenting her right eyebrow. All around adorable.

And very appetizing.

I clear my throat and chuckle.

"How's reading porn going?"

"A Court of Thorn and Roses," she argues, swinging the cover on my nose. "That's not porn!"

"My bad, that's *fairy* porn," I tease on the verge of hilarity, looking at her face turning bright pink with indignation.

"You don't seem to approve, not that I remember asking you."

Brat!

I laugh softly as I continue gazing at her, gloating at her very vexed and very sexy face.

You're just the sweetest thing, aren't you, Princess?

"Nah, my literary expertise in fantasy romance is quite limited, I'm afraid. I'm just surprised is all. I didn't know you were already here. What would you have done if I came in butt naked, flashing my junk at you, poor thing?"

Sophie shrugs her shoulders and fakes an unimpressed look, thinking of a comeback while my thoughts get lost on her neck and then her lips as she passes her tongue over them.

Get a grip, will you?

"I don't know, considering how you're 'dressed' now, you're not leaving much to the imagination either, Dalton."

I offer her a sly smile, nipping my lower lip with my canine.

"The management deeply apologizes and will take good note of your complaint."

"I'm not complaining!"

"Oh, so you like it?" I tease, pulling my pants a little lower.

"That is not what I've said!" she cries.

"What are you saying then?" I whisper, leaning back to her, my breath caressing her chin.

I believe she can probably still smell the sambuca on my breath. She swallows and breathes, closing her sexy eyes. Probably hesitating between slapping me or kissing me, perhaps… I don't know, I assume she's trying to stay in control.

This is way too funny.

Let's take it a little further, shall we?

"Would you like me to kiss you, Sophie?" I whisper again. "Wouldn't you let me give you unfathomable pleasure?"

Her dilated pupils, her slightly open mouth, the soft touch of her hand landing on my arm. I'm sure she can read the gleam of desire that washes over me. She bites her lips and squeezes her thighs again.

I know she wants it.

The door slams in the hallway, and a voice breaks the silence. An all too familiar voice

"Dude, Sophie's already-"

Shit! So soon?

"Yep, mate! I'm aware," I answer, still watching her face. I lean in closer, and with a husk in my voice, I add: "We'll get back to this soon, Princess."

Leaning back up, I walk to the fridge, grab a beer can, and toss it to Miles, smiling at him.

Chapter 2

Sophie

A couple of days had passed since I arrived in London to visit Miles. It was a pleasant change of pace from the tumult of New York City and from my latest exam in my criminal law program. As much as I loved my major, I was more than ready to get that degree and finally move on. Spring break was a big deal, and I'd already had my fair share of Mexican resort debauchery these past few years to fancy a more relaxed week in England before my last semester at Columbia.

It was my chance to spend time with my dearly missed big brother and, well, enjoy the proximity of his eye candy of a roommate.

Our reunion two days prior ended up being much "warmer" than expected. Unsettling, to say the least. There was a time I could hardly look him in the eyes. He haunted so many of my nights and for so long that feeling him so close the other day felt like a dream.

Was it real? Was he really attracted to me, or was it just another one of his jokes?

He used to tease me a lot when I was a teen. Never the way I wished he would, either. After all, I was his best friend's baby sister. But this time got me thinking, he must have been surprised. I mean, I've changed a lot since moving out of our parents' house. To be fair, I am not so little anymore. I've grown, matured, and emancipated. Living on my own gave me all the freedom I wanted to explore many parts of myself, and I thoroughly enjoyed doing so.

At 25, I now know all of my desires, and I am well aware of my dislikes and likes. Needless to say, Dalton is part of the latter, I thought, playing with a strand of hair, contemplating the guest room I am staying in their amazing yet overpriced flat in North London.

Lazily dropping my makeup pouch on the dresser with my brush and straightener, I go over my clothes hanging in the wardrobe, only to fall back down onto the bed.

Hmmpff, so comfy, so warm, I wish some brown-haired someone would come to join me and be the breakfast I need.

"You know you won't be getting anything hotter than coffee? I mumble to myself."

Yup!

A quick look at my phone tells me that it's time to make some bad decisions and break some hearts.

Muffled voices come from the living room. Dalton and Miles must already be up. Jet-lagged as fuck, I finally find the courage to get out of bed after begrudgingly stretching my whole body like a cat. Pulling up my favourite red shorts and black silk top, I emerge from the room, yawning.

"There she is!" exclaims my brother. "How's my favourite Care Bear?"

I shake my head and roll my eyes hearing them. It's kind of early to be dealing with this if you ask me.

"Right back at ya, Bigfoot!" I retort. "But YOU are the hairy one here, and you're in a suspiciously good mood!"

I turn to Dalton.

"Should I be worried?"

"Care Bear? That's a new one, might come in handy later," Dalton sneers, his eyes twinkling with mischief.

My brother places a cup of coffee in front of me and raises a hand, pretending to tousle my hair. I bite the air, falsely threatening. He shrugs.

"My baby sister is here for a whole week, what's not to like?"

"Maybe you should ask Mum and Dad. They weren't too keen on me coming here for my holiday."

Miles snorts and wraps his arms around me, kissing the top of my head.

"Tell me about it," he states. "You're not the one who spent an hour on the phone convincing mummy dearest that her precious princess wouldn't need a nanny to keep her safe!"

I do my best not to cringe too much, but the truth is I'm so over it.

My mother's barely tolerating my very gay brother only in hopes that someday he will change teams, so she'll have a chance to shed some drama tears at a royal wedding reenactment of some sort. Little does she know the wedding extravaganza could one day happen with a blushing bulky, and bearded bride. In the meantime, he gets to increase his body count by a dozen.

Because boys will be boys.

Fucking each other's brains out.

As for me, well, I had to fight tooth and nail just to be able to go study abroad, and it was a nightmare. Every phone call, she never missed pouring on me her what-well-breaded-young-ladies-shouldn't-do-or-say last millennium bullshit. Who would look after me, all alone in that sinful jungle?

Who art to protect thy honor, fair maiden?

I snort at my own joke and shake my head, both hands holding the cup, and take a big sip.

"Mummy dearest should spare me her double standards. You're allowed to fuck every boy that crosses your path."

Miles gasps in shock, but I continue.

"While I should stay at a safe distance from any men that looks my way and lock myself home at all times. And to do what exactly?"

"Masturbate to death, I suppose."

"Yeah… been there, done that, even bought the t-shirt."

"Mum just wants you to be safe," adds my brother.

"Mum would be horrified if she knew half the things I did in New York," I reply with a sly smile.

"Alright, Mata Hari, it's way too early for me. I don't want to hear about your exploits."

"Oh, but I do."

We both turn around to look at Dalton. For a minute, I forgot he was there, listening carefully, flaunting a devilish grin. I take a bow, mischievous. The man, as handsome as usual in his skinny black jeans and Ouija vest, offers a delightful view of his prominent muscles. I fawn and mumble some platitudes about how he, not being my prude mother, might be disappointed, on the other hand, as he appears to be the epitome of the sinful men I should be protected from. He laughs and takes it as a compliment but disagrees as to how boring my experiences could be.

He grins again, his green eyes piercing through my soul, waiting for a reply.

Oh, that's how it is, then?

I wish I could resume our little flirtatious game, but I feel Miles tensing up beside me, ready to go into full protective big bro mode. I sigh, but I really don't mind Dalton's remark, quite the opposite, actually.

We should totally share stories.

"Let's change the subject, shall we?" jokes Bigfoot while I finish my cup of coffee.

"How's work going?"

I continue checking out the sultry roommate while Miles starts talking. An actuary, for the last year or so, he works for a bank in Square Mile, if I recall, or whatever London's business district is. He really enjoys his line of work and passionately explains what the deal is with one of his big clients. As he's yapping away, my cell phone rings. Looking at the ID, I groan.

The Queen Mother sends for me.

Walking away from the guys, I take the call, not because I want to, but because I know that she will leave me alone for a few days if I tell her what she wants to hear. Facing my reflection in the round mirror hanging in the hallway, I blow on the strand of hair falling over my face as I make no effort to carry on the conversation. She admonishes the fact that I chose London over coming home to Yorkshire. I could've been pampered and taken care of. I grimace, her posh voice irritating the life out of me.

Don't worry, mother, someone's gonna take great care of me here, I'm working on it, I thought, glancing over at Dalton. He catches my eye and smirks.

The bastard looks fine.

I pout and concentrate on my mother's yammering again. This call needs to end yesterday. Promising I would text regularly and that I would only go out with Miles and his super queer friends, I finally hang up.

"I need more coffee, bro," I request, being overly dramatic as I hold up my empty cup under his nose.

He trades it for a fresh toast coated with salted butter and turns to the coffee pot for my refill. I thank him and stretch over the table to grab some jelly. My hand hovers a moment above the jar as I catch a leer weaving down into my top.

I feel fire starting on my neck and cheeks as I know he can clearly see, well, everything.

He whispers, "Now that's what I call not leaving much to the imagination, Princess."

"You need to shut up!"

"What I need… is a shower," suddenly declares the rocker, pulling off his vest.

Fuck me!

I eye him as every muscle flexes on his body. This man is out of this world.

"Really, Dalton? Streaking in front of my pure and innocent baby sister?" goofs Miles, pretending to block the view.

"Pure and innocent, hmm? I doubt she feels the same. Am I right, Soph?"

"Purity is a product of patriarchy."

"See?" Dalton points out to my brother. "I have known Sophie for the past ten years, mate. She was innocent then, but now I don't think she minds if I don't wear a top," he retorts, turning towards me, his brow raised, a wicked grin playing on his lips.

"Your place your rules, I guess. You can walk naked if you want, I wouldn't bat an eye," I reply nonchalantly while, on the contrary, my insides furiously ignite.

The disapproving pout Miles serves me makes me snort, but it's smarter not to engage now. I walk away, still drooling over Dalton's abs, and sit on the armchair in the corner.

"When will the gang be here?" asks the long hair demigod licking his luscious lips.

"Around 5:30, mate. We're going to have a few drinks and then order in."

"And what will we order?" I question excitedly.

Please be Indian food, please be Indian food!

"Indian."

"Yes!!" I applaud. "I haven't had any in a few months, this is great!"

"Are we sticking with poker as well?" interrogates Miles.

Dalton nods and cracks his knuckles, groaning. The sounds reverberate deeply into my core. I swear I will get this man, or help me, God.

The bastard knows all too well the power he holds over me. He is torturing me on purpose and enjoying it way too much!

I would have him kneel and beg if I wasn't too keen on kneeling before him myself. I blink and refrain from the visions rushing to my mind of flesh slamming against each other.

Pure and innocent, my ass!

I pull out my phone and turn away, scrolling through my emails in hopes of hiding the thoughts traveling at light speed across my face.

"I think so, not sure," adds Dalton. "Maybe we should play a board game. I wouldn't want to steal all of Soph's money nor her clothes."

"She doesn't have to play."

"You realize I'm sitting right here, right Bigfoot? I'm pretty capable of handling anything Dalton comes at me with!"

I instantly realized the words came out too fast and not in the sense I intended! I bite my tongue way too late as the heat flushes up from my neck to my hair.

"What's that you say, sis? You're a little red in the face, aren't you?"

"Your mother, the whore!" I shriek, hiding behind a cushion.

Dalton chuckles and gets up, offering me a lovely view of his tall frame and firm behind. My thoughts trail again despite being already so obvious, and I imagine myself digging my nails into his lower back while he violently pounds deeply into me.

Gazing at me, he walks away, waving his hand, leaving me with my fantasy.

"Be good kids! Try not to kill each other while Daddy's away!"

Miles shakes his head, looking at me with a shit-eating grin as Dalton leaves the room. Waiting for the shower to be running, he exclaims, "Get your mind out of the gutter, Sophie!"

"What are you on about?" I innocently question.

"I saw how you are drooling all over him. Little sis, it's not a good idea. It's not really my story to tell, but Dalton had his fair share of heartaches, so he hasn't been dating in a long while."

Surprised, I don't really know what to say to that. It never occurred to me that the object of my desires could be vulnerable.

"I am not looking to marry the guy, Miles, just to have mind-blowing consensual sex for a night or two."

My brother cringes, wraps his arms around me, and squeezes me tightly.

"Just be careful, okay? I want to save my favourite Care Bear from heartache."

"You're such a softy," I laugh, cupping his face with my hands. "I promise I won't hurt his little heart."

"Nor yours."

"Copy that." I give him a mock two-fingered salute.

***

Holding a glass, sitting among Miles' friends, I'm enjoying myself, basking in the warmth, gleeful conversations, good spirits, and infectious laughs. My brother's entourage is smart, nice, and super cute!

"Fischer, I must say your sister is a gem! Where were you hiding her all this time?" Interrogates Charles, a tall blonde-haired bearded guy who's totally my brother's type.

"At Columbia, New York Citaaay," replies my brother, with the most over-exaggerated American accent he could muster.

"Well, excuse moi! What are you studying?" He continues with a broad smile that lights up all of his face. "No, no, no, let me guess… fashion?"

"Criminal Law."

The group burst into laughter at Charles.

"A lawyer can come in handy someday," replies Joseph, his hair dishevelled surrounding his angelic face.

"Don't be too eager to make use of my skills. I still have to pass the bar first," I wink at him, taking a sip of my almost empty drink.

I sigh and glance at the kitchen where Dalton's helping Nadia mix drinks. While pouring quite a heavy amount of Captain Morgan into a shaker, he's chewing on a toothpick, flipping it between his lips from time to time. I can't take my eyes off his mouth and the oh-so-inspiring toothpick twirling.

That's a skill that might come in handy.

Feeling flushed once more, I clear my throat.

I smile and nod at a work-related joke that my brother's telling a captivated and already won-over audience. From my understanding,

Nadia, the little pink-haired girl bartending with Dalton in the kitchen, and Joseph work with him restoring old boats, while Charles is the drummer in their alternative rock band.

The more the evening passed, the more I learned interesting things about Dalton. Woodwork and guitar, which explains his robust and calloused hands.

The group of friends seems pretty solid and caring with each other, and it's comforting to see my brother thriving amongst them.

I don't know when they came to be "the gang," though I vaguely remember seeing Jo with Dalton and Miles many years ago. I finish my glass and walk in to see if I can help with anything.

"May I be of any use to you guys? Perhaps, trade places with you, Nadia?"

"Don't mind if I do, lovely," she replies gracefully.

"Fetch me more ice, Princess, will you?" asks Dalton, unfazed.

"Jeez…" I whistle. "We're getting bossy, are we? Y'know, a 'please' wouldn't hurt!"

"Little girl, you better do as I say."

"Or else?" I fawn.

Dalton stops and tilts his head, the little wooden stick flipping between his teeth as he refrains with a somehow predatory smile.

He slowly turns and steps towards me, his face almost hovering over mine.

His eyes, as green as the ocean riveted to mine at first, gaze down to my lips and lower again before catching up my eyes again, intense, inviting me to look at something down there. I hold my breath, tingles running down my spine.

Now is not the time nor the place for…

He glances down again. An invitation. A silent order. I stare at him, open mouth, burning eyes, unsure about what to do.

Hesitantly I dare to look down to see… an empty bucket in his hands. I step back, facing his voracious smile.

"Ice, *pl-ease,*" he articulates.

The same ice I feel flushing over my head as I hop back into reality and try to save whatever composure I have left.

"Yes, sir!" I say, placing my shaking hand on my forehead as a salute to him.

He laughs frankly, and even though I'm kinda mortified, it's literally music to my ears. Stepping to the fridge, I grab some ice and put a small cube in my mouth. I crunch on it to cool down a bit and bring the bucket back to him. I run a hand through my hair and lean on the counter as he mixes alcohol with colourful soft drinks.

"Would you like to try one?" he asks in a sultry tone.

"Yeah, why not?" I mutter, my heart still pounding from before.

He places himself behind me as I start pouring Captain Morgan into the glasses. Hints of musk and spices hit my nose as he puts his hands on each side of me.

I would love for time to stop right now. There's no need for him to stand this way to show me how to mix rum and fucking orange juice. He's playing, establishing dominance, punishing me somehow for my sassiness earlier, knowing it will drive me to the edge.

Warmth wraps around me. His hair slowly falls over my shoulders. I close my eyes feeling his hot breath on me, and it takes every bit of strength I have, not to turn around and hide my face in his neck.

The metallic tinkling of the ice falling in the glasses calls me back to reality.

Drinks, I am mixing drinks.

"Think you might be able to carry on, Princess?" he whispers in my ear.

"Easy peasy, Captain!" My voice squeaking much more than I wish.

"Okay then," he retorts, walking out of the room, leaving me cold and frustrated.

"You fancy him, don't you?"

I turn around to see Nadia leaning on the counter.

"Someone's curious," I laugh, handing her a drink.

She shrugs and tilts her head while eyeing Dalton.

"Well, for what it's worth, you should totally go for it."

Oh, love, I am working on it...

Nodding, I watch her take the remaining glasses to the table, where she is applauded and cheered for by the boys. Dalton joins me back, a cigarette between his lips.

"You're not drinking with them?"

"Nah, I just wanted a breather," I smile.

"Care to join me?" he asks, showing his lighter and pack of cigarettes.

I nod again and follow him outside. The night is clear, and the air is fresh, charged with fragrant cut grass and humidity.

Dalton sits on the stairs and runs a hand through his hair before lighting his fag.

He inhales the smoke, glancing at me.

I sit next to him, my arms wrapped around my knees. We stay silent for a while, listening to the murmur of the city.

"You okay, Princess?" he asks.

"Social interactions can be a bit much for me," I explain, looking at the starless sky. "I wouldn't say I can't stand the company of humans too long, but... yeah."

He chuckles in the dark.

"Tell me, Dalton, that trick with the toothpick, does it really help you land the ladies?"

He pauses and frowns, confused.

"Pardon?"

"That thing you did earlier... spinning the toothpick with your tongue like it's a bloody twirling baton?"

He smirks and exhales smoke up.

"Why? Is it working?" He leans closer to me.

Ass...

"That's merely a nervous tic. You're the first one to notice, I'm afraid."

"So... no trick then."

"Sorry to disappoint," he smiles contritely.

"Never!"

I shiver in the cool night breeze and rub my nose against my sleeve. Staring at the empty street, I ponder out loud.

"It's easy for you, isn't it?"

"What do you mean?"

"What's it like to be that good-looking and get whomever you fancy?"

Dalton shakes his head, his eyes still looking into mine. I perceive sadness in them for the first time, which makes me frown. Maybe this is what Miles was telling me about earlier.

"If you only knew Soph… Let's just say that I'm confidently average, and I know what I can work with."

"You, average?!" I scoff and nudge him. "What does that make me then?"

"Hot, sweet, very desirable? Choices are yours. I'm comfortable with what I am, and that's fine," he winks at me. "Don't try and overthink this, Princess."

He crushes his half-smoked cigarette under his shoe and stands up.

"You're right about humans, though," he smiles tenderly, giving me his hands to help me get up. "Very few are worth your company."

Later as the night unfolds and the group gets fashionably drunk, I find myself getting more confident as to what I am hungry for. Surprises, adventures, and for now, naans and an otherworldly Tikka Masala chicken!

As amazing as I remember it!

The dinner table covered with boxes steaming delicious spice perfumes, sitting around, we share embarrassing stories of our childhoods. I feel light-headed and happy, the alcohol dancing through my bloodstream. I feel good. Uninhibited. Free. Horny.

Naughty, naughty me.

Looking at Dalton, I smile in the blur of dim lights and buzzing conversations around me. Oblivious of me, shamelessly leering down at his statuesque beauty, he's listening to Charles while running his thumb on his lips. I can't help but imagine how it must be to kiss him.

Why don't you just ask him that?

As I open my mouth, Jo's communicative laugh bursts by my side and shakes this idea out of me.

"Ladies, we'll get the table ready for poker. Would you fix a few more drinks in the meantime?" politely asks Charles.

"On it!" replies Nadia. "No need to measure anymore. I think we're all good," laughs the petite woodworker.

"Might be right there," I concede.

"So, are you ready for poker?" she continues.

"As much as one can be, I believe. I think they will destroy me, though."

Nads laughs and finishes mixing the last drink.

"You'll be fine, love; I am sure Dalton will have your back," she winks and walks back to the table.

"Oh, he can have my back and everything else," I mutter, plunging my nose in some orange and rum, also known as ass-kicking liquid courage.

Poker is all about risks, and I decide whether I'm bad at cards, I will take my chances elsewhere. Sitting right beside Dalton, I grin and grab a few chips to help absorb the alcohol. Charles explains the ground rules, under the clamours of Dalton and Jo booing in unison, that we will only play for money.

Worry not…

O Captain! My Captain! Rise up and hear… the sound of my underwear… evaporating.

Coming to jokes, I'm my best audience, I think, gloating as I fail to resist gravity and lean towards Dalton. On the other side of the table, my brother is looking at me, but at this point, I don't really care anymore.

Not so steady, I cross my legs, wishing to put Sharon Stone to shame, and failing again, miserably, I end up grovelling on my not-impressed neighbour.

"Oh, sorry, look at me taking all of the space."

He leans, detailing me, and whispers.

"Don't lie to yourself, Soph. You know you can't help touching me."

"Keep dreaming," I stutter. "You're not t-that hot."

"Says the one who's playing footsie with me under the table."

"You'd know if I was, Dalton," I reply with a cheeky smile.

"Oh really?"

I nod, grinning even more.

"That's good to know, Princess, might come in handy soon."

"Oh, someone's got a foot fetish?"

"I'm a depraved manwhore, longing to lure innocent souls into debauchery, remember? My fetish tastes measure up to my reputation…"

"Meaning?" I gag, squeezing my thigh to stay in control.

He smiles voraciously.

"You won't be able to resist me."

"Bold of you to assume it won't be the other way round."

Troubled by the exchange, I stare at my cards like I know what I'm doing and ask for two more while I discard a pair of fours. This is the exact moment Jo chooses to let me know I shouldn't play so fast since it's the best way to lose.

"You WILL lose, Princess," purrs Dalton in my ear.

No way I'm letting him get away with this one!

"Lose? I don't recall betting on anything…"

"Would you?"

"Well, my father always told me in bets there's a fool and a liar, so… which one are you?"

The devil stays silent, the tension thickening as Dalton's grin enlarges.

"That's a snarky one…"

"I have my moments…"

"And you always listen to your *Daddy*?"

"I'll have you know I'm known to be a disobedient brat," I smirk. "Besides, a game only really becomes interesting when there's a prize, don't you agree?"

"I can think of one…"

I press my thighs together and bite my lip as he groans dangerously close to my neck.

"We'll see about that, won't we?" I say without much confidence.

"Royal flush!!!" calls out Miles, drunk as a skunk, breaking our bubble. "I win, suckers!" he gloats.

My brother takes the cash on the table while Dalton offers me another drink, his arm now leaning on my chair, warm against my shoulders. Goosebumps and chills darting my skin over my whole body. I close my eyes for a second, relishing the lovely sensation, leaning back on him, making as much contact as possible. I side-glance at him after taking one of my sandals off as I start to rub his ankle with my bare foot. A thin smile stretches his lips as he suggests a toast.

A warm feeling spreads against the soft skin of my thigh as I look down to see his hand, which had left my back, brushing it delicately.

"Tut, tut, tut, Princess, you know what they say when people don't look in each other's eyes while they toast…"

"That they will get 7 years of the worst sex ever," I reply, blushing.

"Let's hope that doesn't happen to us," he smirks, pinching slightly my shivering skin.

"150 quid!! That's what I'm talking about," exclaims my brother, ruining the mood for good.

For Christ's sake!!!

The laughs keep coming as Miles, in a blaze of glory and totally trashed, is now murdering Gloria Gaynor's life work singing at the top of his lungs, "Can't take my eyes off of you." The angry pounding of the upstairs neighbours signals the end of the night, and as I bid good night to the gang and start cleaning, Dalton has to take my reluctant intoxicated mess of a brother to his bed.

Not too long passes before I hear footsteps coming back behind me.

"We're the last ones standing!"

"Did you have fun, Princess?" interrogates Dalton.

"I did… the singing number was a bit too much, though."

No answer but the warmth of his chest against my back. His hands landing on my hips. He brushes the skin on my neck with his lips, and I can imagine the smirk he has when I can't refrain from a moan.

"That's more my kind of music."

I close my eyes and let my head rest against his shoulder.

Oh, please don't stop. Go on.

His hands slipping under my blouse, firming their hold on my flesh, his lips caressing my neck again, he pauses and smiles, nibbling the edge of my ear.

"Let the games continue, Princess…" he whispers as he slowly pulls away. "Goodnight, Sophie."

Chapter 3

Dalton

"Went out shopping, text me if you need anything before I get back."

The little note, decorated with hideous butterflies, has me smiling. Sophie's handwriting is as preppy as her. That girl's been here for less than a week and has already filled our days with sunshine and mother fucking butterflies, I think, throwing my keys and jacket on the couch.

What could I need from her?

A couple of days had passed since poker night, and I can't really say that the tension between Sophie and I has calmed down. We kept our little game going whenever we were in each other's company. A light touch here, a few dirty words there. I was getting pretty frustrated in the most exhilarating way.

Tired, I stand in the living room. Calm. My imagination still wandering around, thinking of all the ways we could give in and end this game. I grin to myself as I stretch towards the ceiling.

I can't wait to see how this turns out.

Sunlight filters through the window, warming up the room. It makes me think that summer's just around the corner. Some vacations would be very much appreciated, I ponder, exhausted by this morning's shift.

I look at my dry and calloused hands, suddenly thinking how much I'd like to touch something soft and tender for a change.

Like a silk top falling to the floor, red hair, and velvety skin.

Lust and weariness make you dangerously sentimental, mate!

Miles and Sophie being out, I have the place all to myself. Taking my shirt off, I stand some more in the warmth of the sun heating up the window. Job was a bore today, but I have a few days off from the workshop, and I intend to make the most of it. I can concentrate a bit more on my music and that cheeky little vixen.

As fun as it is to be lazy, I pour myself some fresh hot coffee and pick up my guitar, my notebook as well as a pen. For reasons unknown to me, I have been feeling very inspired recently.

Yeah, right, reasons unknown.

Basking in the soft glow, I sit by the window, gripping the cords of my guitar. With the pen between my lips, I conjure up a melody.

It's been a while since music came that easy. I lean back in the chair and breathe deeply, closing my eyes. Nothing else exists anymore. I feel good. Relaxed. Powerful. Lost in my thoughts, images vibrating through my mind, I imagine my hands, my lips caressing the soft skin of the girl I admire as much as I desire, and sentences start forming in my head.

I have got to write this down.

I tie my hair up and remove the pen from the grip of my teeth before I start writing as the lyrics keep coming to me, flowing as I lay them down in my notebook. I read them back, scratch a few words, shaping them along the lines of my very graphic thoughts until I am mostly satisfied. After a few hours, I have a new song.

Not bad... not bad at all.

I'll have to run it by Charles at some point. His insights never miss improving my drafts. I crack my neck and knuckles and check the time on my phone. They should get back soon, might as well start dinner. I get up, untie my hair and walk into the kitchen. Hearing the front door opening, I casually lean forward and open the fridge.

"About damn time!" I chuckle, grabbing chicken and veggies.

Miles dramatically puts his hand on his forehead and sighs.

"This little one wanted to buy everything from that Hell Rabbit clothing store," he explains, exhausted.

"Hell Bunny."

"Whatever! It was all vintage pinup frill and petticoats!"

"Lucky for you, I am THAT kind of Goth and didn't drag you down Camden to Cyberdog!" she adds, irritated.

"You wouldn't dare!"

"Try me!"

"Are you two going to shut it already?" I interject.

Miles gasps again, flipping me off while Sophie rolls her eyes and goes to drop her bags in her room. I hear her footsteps skipping down the stairs as she returns.

"So, what are you cooking for us, Dalton?" She inquires, pushing a strand of hair behind her ear.

"Chicken fajitas, olé!" I reply, shaking my hips clumsily, which makes her laugh.

"Hey, bud!" I shout, tossing the onions at Miles. "Let's get chopping."

The atmosphere is light, and I even manage to cook everything without burning down the house.

Cheers!

After some discussion about a hypothetical risk of food poisoning due to my fine cuisine from the two siblings, I finally get them to sit and eat! We laugh, we tease each other, Sophie flirts, Miles groans, and opens a bottle of wine.

The dinner's done, I clean the dishes with the redhead as my roommate picks up a conference call in his office. Looking down at her, I smirk.

"You realize you don't have to be so smug all the time, right?" she starts as she puts a plate away in the cupboard, as my gaze roams her body.

I tone it down a notch.

"It's my natural state, Princess."

Her piercing eyes search for mine. Sharp. Calling me on my bullshit.

"It's almost like you always try to hide your true self from others. Or at least from me, that makes you -"

"Dark and mysterious?"

"Distant and asshole-ish,"

"Ouch! Put your claws away, Kitten."

"That didn't come out right. Just, you're funny and creative," she adds, pointing at my guitar. "Why do I feel like you gate-keep your emotions?"

"To prevent little minxes like you to get too close and burn their curious little whiskers!"

"Or to prevent *you* from getting hurt?"

Yeah…

"You won't let that one go, right, Princess?"

"I'm a feisty little brat, remember?"

I nod.

"You know, I'm not drunk enough for pillow talk," I whisper, looking down at her while her mercurial irises probe deep into my soul.

"Miles talked a little about your last relationship," she continues as I groan and make a mental note to kick my bud's ass later. "Not everything always has to be a game."

"Who says I'm playing games all the time?"

I am straightforward. Dates are a no-go for me. I don't lie or hide things. Everyone I get involved with clearly knows I am emotionally unavailable. And now Sophie does too. I concentrate on her inquisitive face again.

"Wouldn't you like to build something strong with someone one day?" she asks.

"Not really, no," I say, tracing the outline of my forearm tattoo with my finger. "I don't believe that you need to be in a relationship to be happy in life. You know it's all fun and games until someone gets hurt."

She nods as she listens and chews on her cheek, which is probably one of the cutest things I have seen her do so far.

"That's fair enough, Dalton, but everyone deserves to be loved."

"Maybe I'm not made for it, and it's fine, Princess. Best case scenario, it happens, and that's a bonus." I conclude, watching the water drain down into the sink.

***

Laying on my bed, I look at the white ceiling. My earlier conversation with Sophie has stayed with me. "Everyone deserves to be loved." not everyone, no, love is a scam. Being confidently average, I somehow managed so far to seduce my fair share of women. My "body count" is probably not as impressive as Sophie's mother or Sophie herself might imagine, though.

Come to think of it, the number is not as interesting as their diversity. I don't particularly have a type, I'm only interested in one thing: chemistry. A look, a scent, a detail spicy enough to light a spark of curiosity, as long as their personality meshes well with mine, I'm good to go.

In more ways than one.

I chuckle, pulling my inverted cross earring. My mind starts wandering again. Sophie's angelic face floating over mine. The vision of her perky breasts bouncing as my hands grip her flesh, leaving my mark on it.

Fuck!

The tightness I feel in my trousers is a good reminder to make some decisions about this whole chasing game. I can't pretend indifference anymore. She got her way inside my head, under my skin, and I will have to deal with this, or I might end up going completely crazy.

Exhaling deeply, I look down at my lower parts, man now is not the time. We'll have that conversation later in the shower, shall we?

Might as well sweat it off instead; I haven't been to the gym in a couple of days. What better way to clear up tension than doing a little training?

I strip the clothes off my back and stare at my reflection in my cracked mirror. Cracked, not broken, just like me, seven years of bad luck can wait.

I judge my progress pretty harshly, though my younger, skinny self would be shocked at how we got good at calisthenics and how we grew some muscles. Yet here I am bitching about my results and my forever work-in-progress six-pack, squinting at the lower line, still not as defined as I would like it to be.

I blast some music to get the rhythm while I drag the dip training bars in the middle of the room. Animals by Architects starts flowing out of the speakers right through me as I take a deep breath in and stretch out.

Gripping the black steel bars, I push my whole body up and down until beads of sweat start forming on my forehead, and all my muscles are burning. The pain spreads from my tightened core to the tips of my fingers, but I love how it makes me feel.

Fucking alive!

Pain, pleasure, the two mixed together.

Control and surrender.

These are the ones I seek, above love.

A fluttering shadow gets my attention. From the corner of my eye, I realize I am being observed.

Well, well, what do we have here?

I wonder if she's enjoying the view. Of course, she is. The hornier she gets, the more reckless she's getting. Her intentions are pretty clear at this point. She might as well start touching herself right then and there.

Let's push this a little further.

I stop for a minute holding the pose, offering my best flex to her as I growl like an animal. I'd like it so much if I could just hear her squeak. I get on the ground and work some push-ups out, groaning much more than I usually do. From what I can see, it's working. Her silhouette's twitching, squeezing her arms, crossing her legs, probably biting her lips till she bleeds.

I grin, mischievous, and keep going at it.

Come on, Princess, let go. I know you can't stand it anymore. What are you waiting for? My permission?

Some delicious shivers of anticipation make my cock twitch. Hmm, do what I say, not what I do. I get a few more reps done and get back up. Dripping in sweat, I can imagine how she sees my glistening skin.

Now both of us are wet, aren't we?

Why not go all the way?

For my final move, something a tad more sensual. Irresistible. I go down a warpath, scorched earth, and shit as the song changes to Pony, heavy beats start blaring, and I slam myself down the floor, pounding it for dear life.

Sophie bursts into laughter, "For fuck's sake Dalton," she cries. "You're taking the piss?"

I nod, laughing so hard that I roll onto my back, gripping my already aching sides.

"You knew I was here the whole time, didn't you?"

"Took you long enough to notice," I smile as she rolls her eyes.

Sitting up, I beckon her over with one finger. She sits down next to me, and I change the music and look at her.

"I made you come with one finger," I say, wiping my face. "Imagine what I could do with two."

"You're enjoying yourself, aren't you?"

"Do you mean in general?"

"No," she replies. "I mean when you are tormenting me."

"Oh, that? Well, yeah!" I answer with a big ass grin lighting up my face as her pretty little eyes devour me with lust.

We talk a little more. She deflects what I guess is an embarrassment with compliments over my looks and what she calls my Cirque du Soleil performance. She pouts when I reply that I'm impervious to flattery, and I stand by looking confidently average.

As to Cirque du Soleil, I never had any complaints about my performances, but I doubt they would care as they are mostly NSFW.

However, I do enjoy the way her face contorts when she is annoyed. I can't help myself; whenever she is around me, I feel the urge to tease her, and her reactions never disappoint.

"Time for a shower," I say, leaning towards her. "Care to join me?"

She holds my gaze and shakes her head, looking like a deer caught in headlights.

"I'm not that easy, Captain!"

I hear a tremble in her voice.

"I've heard that before, Princess."

She shrugs and crosses her arms.

"Your loss," I reply, getting up, watching in the mirror, her eyes dropping down my body and locking on to the bulge in my grey joggers. "Now be a good girl and go fix Daddy a drink while I get cleaned up."

She scoffs and flips me off.

"Easy on the smartassery. You wouldn't want me to put you in the naughty corner now, would you?"

I laugh, seeing her cheeks flush red while I imagine what could be running in her precious little mind.

Don't worry, Kitten, I'll take care of you soon enough...

Chapter 4

Sophie

"…meaning that we could differentiate Procedural Justice, which concerns the mechanism by which decisions are made in opposition, as Substantive Justice which is more concerned with the end result. In conclusion…"

I sigh and groan as I finally reach the end of the damn dissertation I should have finished on the plane.

The obsessive and nervous tapping of my own fingers on the keyboard filling the room was starting to get what was left of my patience.

That fucking paper got me bored out of my mind.

I dance around in the living room, blissfully free of my obligations, struck by the implacable truth: I have no idea what to do with myself. Too much tension building up inside of me; boredom, hunger, and a quite persistent feeling of dissatisfaction that has me spiralling. I need to find something to do, to pass the time and end this torture.

Like a run.

Or filthy, disheveling, back-breaking sex.

But as for the latter, I'm reliant on other vectors, I think, biting my cheek, still beating myself up for turning down Dalton's offer.

It's not that simple.

No shit!

Of course, it is! You're both adults, obviously consenting, why are you having second thoughts?

The answer is 6'5 and in a Teams meeting next door. My brother's working from home this afternoon, and as much as I love him, I do not wish to deal with him at the moment.

The thought of him barging in on Dalton and I going at it or just imagining him hearing whatever noises I'd make, and I know for a fact I would be uncontrollably vocal... absolutely fucking not!

I sit on the couch only to get up immediately. I'm too restless. Dalton has upped his game. Now in a constant state of want and need, my own fingers aren't enough anymore. I need to do something, or I might explode.

A ruffle in the kitchen has me jumping out of my skin.

"What are you doing, Care Bear?" asks my brother, looking suspiciously at my probably guilty face, while preparing himself a sandwich.

"Not sure yet," I reply, grabbing an apple. "I think I'm going to go for a run in Trent Park. It will help with the pent-up energy I have."

"Brilliant!"

"Are you trying to get rid of me, Miles?"

He chuckles and boops my nose.

"I would never, but I do think getting out of the house will do you good."

I nod and kiss his cheek before going into my room. I dig around my clothes and grab a pink pair of leggings and a white shirt before grabbing my earbuds and choosing Dalton's playlist, which I shamelessly hunted for on Spotify. I wave at Miles as I pass him by and step out of the flat. I close my eyes and breathe deeply as I stretch my legs a little. The music blasting in my ears instantly reminds me of what Dalton was working out to yesterday. I press skip, annoyed, mostly at myself for not being able to get him out of my head, but then I guess I am just a glutton for punishment.

I am a grown woman; he shouldn't get to me as easily as he did when we were kids. However, the truth is, I like the way he looks at me; he makes me feel wanted and special.

I cross my arms, stretching my shoulders.

I like how he makes me feel, then again, he's a major flirt; it's part of the game, making every girl feel unique. He knows what he's selling, dreams, an unforgettable night, and no promises. I realize that I really like that about him, knowing that deep down, he isn't the heartless fuckboy he pretends to be. I feel privileged to have seen more of him, of his heart.

I hope my brother will go out on a date with Charles soon or whomever he will find on Grindr so I can finally be alone with Dalton before going back to New York.

"You wouldn't want to be put in the naughty corner now, would you?"

His voice still follows me as I walk towards Middlesex University, leading my steps and my fantasy away.

"What would you want to punish me for, Daddy?"

"You, little brat, have been a bad girl and need to be taught some manners."

My whole body aches just thinking about it.

"You think so?"

"I know so, now say it!"

"I've been a bad girl, Daddy."

The story unfolds in my head as I am convinced that he would be able to satisfy every and all of my untold desires. I'm hopeless, craving for the lust this man oozes from every pore. A shiver running down my spine, I wish to let myself go in his grip. Under his perfectly controlled hands, I can imagine how good he really is with his fingers.

My strides are light and smooth, but I feel my body heating. He consumes me to the point where I am having a really hard time just focusing and keeping myself occupied.

I turn right on Snakes Lane and speed up towards the Southgate Hockey Center. I cross paths with other joggers and tourists, and I get why this place is gorgeous. The sun shines high in the sky, and it's the perfect weather to get some air and clear one's head!

I keep running towards the red brick building while drops of sweat start rolling down my forehead, contouring my temples and my cheeks and dripping from under my jaw. I keep my strides steady as I start feeling my lungs burning.

Use it as a thing to focus on, dammit!

I'm getting mad at myself. Even though I have been running for the past hour, I'm still haunted by Dalton. His luscious lips, his long dark hair. How I wish I could entangle my fingers in it. The green of his eyes, the veins of his toned arms, his abs, his obliques, and the thin hairline pointing to his...

Son of a bitch!

I trip, miss a stride, and almost fall flat on my ass.

Ok, time to go back home before someone gets hurt!

You, bitch, need an ice-cold shower!

I skip the songs until I find one with a nice rhythm that will help me pace back to Miles' place. With the music helping, I manage to cool down and head back without any incident.

Thank goodness.

Once inside the flat, I remove and throw my shoes in the corner of the hallway and take off my soggy shirt before walking into the kitchen. I open the fridge to cool myself off as much as to find something to drink that isn't alcohol.

Dudes, really?

I finally grasp an untouched bottle of orange juice.

"Ew, my little sister's naked," cries out Miles behind me.

"Calm down drama queen!" I reply after downing half the bottle. "It's like you never saw a woman in a sports bra."

I giggle. He rolls his eyes dramatically and mimics my laugh.

"Very, VERY funny, Soph! You stink, though, so please go wash yourself," he says before adding. "And don't forget to call Mother. She has been harassing me all afternoon."

"Yeah, yeah, yeah, will do."

I present him with my best sarcastic smile, finish my juice and drag myself to the bathroom. Taking off my clothes, I take a long look at myself in the mirror. I imagine Dalton's eyes following the curves of my thighs, going up to my breasts as I cup them up provocatively, trying to make them appear bigger, biting my lower lip in a horny, ingenue, submissive, yet seductive way.

Holy Dakota Johnson, you look stupid!

I shake my head, smiling at my foolishness, and step into the shower, closing the curtain behind me.

A really cold shower, that's what you need.

I turn it on and bite my lips, sealed for real, as the freshwater falls over my heating body. I keep a moan of surprise in, and after a few seconds of cold showering, I switch back to warm water.

I'm finally able to close my eyes and relax under the high-pressure jet while I think about New York. It will be the last stretch before my internship at Raiser & Kenniff, one of the best criminal law firms. My parents are very proud of my career choice, the firstborn being an actuary, they wouldn't appreciate their daughter choosing something other than a liberal profession, even though, they never got how I could be so interested in crimes.

Completely lost in my thoughts, I jumped when the shower suddenly switched back to cold. This time's not my fault, I think, hearing water running from the bathroom sink.

"For fuck's sake, Miles, it's freezing! You know I'm in here. Turn it off!"

The water stops, and a low chuckle replies.

Fuck me!!! It's Dalton!

"I'm starting to think that I really have to teach you some manners, Princess."

I smile to myself.

Game on.

"Oh, and how are you planning to do that?" I reply with the most cynical, mocking tone I can think of.

"I'm not sure yet, but you can bet I will get an eyeful before going back to my room," he retorts, laughing.

"How 'bout no?"

"Why would I not? You've been eyeing me for the past week, thinking I wasn't seeing it. It's my turn now," he whispers in a husky, silky voice.

"You weren't fully naked, though." I ponder as I open the curtain just enough to show my face and greet him with a murderous glare.

"Who do you think you're trying to impress, Kitten? I can perfectly figure how you look under your clothes without even having to look at you."

I furiously blush and close the curtain back, which makes him laugh again.

What should I blush for? Dalton just admit...

"Are you, Sir, implying you have undressed me in your mind? Am I haunting your dreams too?"

"I said what I said."

I smile, finishing rinsing the soap off my skin while Dalton does God knows what. Only a few more minutes, he will leave, and I'll be alone again. I gasp when I hear knocking on the door.

"Care Bear, I have to brush my teeth and grab my watch. I'm going out with Charles and running late. I will be quick, promise."

You've got to be fucking kidding me.

I open the curtain again, and without thinking, I grip the demigod's shirt and drag him into the bathtub with me. I push him against the wall and make him lean forward so I can put my hand over his mouth. Dalton is dying of laughter, but I implore him to be silent.

"Come in, Miles, but make it fast," I anxiously shriek. My voice is strained and unsure.

Could I be more obvious?

The door opens, and my brother comes in.

Don't talk, please don't talk, I pray, as much for my brother than for his roommate, who is now eyeing me with lust and something I can't quite put my finger on. Of course, while I was panicking, I completely forgot that I was naked. I kindly slap him and force him to look me in the eyes.

"Enjoy your evening Soph," shouts my over-enthusiastic brother. "I think Dalton's out, I haven't seen him in a while."

"I wouldn't know. I haven't seen him either," I blatantly lie, looking at the culprit dead in the eye.

"Don't wait up for me," he adds, snorting.

I nod, still staring at Dalton like a psycho.

"I should be able to find something interesting to occupy myself with. Have a good night!"

Miles finally leaves the bathroom, and we are alone again. I exhale while my hostage raises a cocky eyebrow as I feel a smirk forming against my palm. Slowly, he takes off my hand from his mouth and slides it onto his muscular chest. Without taking his eyes off of me, he caresses my wrist, ascending to the fold of my elbow with his fingers. I shiver, covering my breasts with my other arm. Pointless now, he has really seen everything. I realize I'm shaking.

Coming off the wall, he steps forward, pushing me back under the shower.

"What are you doing, Dalton? You're already soaking wet."

With a half smile on his lips, he towers over me, exposing us to the warm shower jets. Time stops as I observe, mesmerized, the water running over his face, dripping from his jaw, and contouring his chest. I feel like I'm looking at a movie in slow motion, the way he slicks his long hair back while his white vest sticks to his defined and chiseled body. Every detail of his features is burned into my mind as the drops of water form little pearls on his long eyelashes, the tip of his nose, and the curve of his inviting mouth.

His mouth.

"Come on, get out, what are you waiting for?" I ask in a trembling voice.

"Are you sure it's really what you want, Princess?"

I shake my head. Of course, I don't want him out, I am naked, and he's all wet, his now transparent shirt looking thermobonded to his torso so perfectly it could be Photoshopped! Of course, I want more of it!

The steam clogs the bathroom, blurring the contour of the room. As in a dream, my shaky hands run on his chest. Under my fingers, the cotton of his vest rasps, heavy and damp. I finally touch the warmth and silky skin of his neck. Pushing myself on my tiptoes, I grab his nape and draw him towards me. I'm not shaking anymore, I'm hungry, hungry for him. I crash into him, as my lips finally find his.

The effect is immediate.

His damp hair sticks to my skin, his hands gripping hard into my flesh, caressing me more and more urgently, making me completely lose myself. It's as good, no better, than what I had imagined. Thousands of butterflies flutter around in my stomach as Dalton slides his tongue inside my mouth and searches for mine. Goosebumps fill my skin, and a small electric shock gets to my heart.

I am kissing my secondary school crush.

I smile against his mouth at the thought and lean back. Panting, my long-haired sex dream of a man caresses my cheeks with his thumbs before kissing me again. A delicate, heartfelt, and sensual kiss. Softer this time, but somehow with greater conviction.

I regain my senses before things get fully out of hand, even though we're both pretty excited at this point. I put a hand on his chest, looking up at him.

"I think the coast is clear now," I say, putting an arm over my bare breasts.

"To be continued…" he whispers.

He smiles and kisses my forehead before getting out of the shower. I hear him taking off his clothes and putting them in the dryer before taking a towel. My heart practically beating out of my chest, I wait for him to get out to turn off the shower and start breathing again.

What am I supposed to do now?

Chapter 5

Dalton

Sitting on the edge of my bed, I run a thumb over my lips, the taste of her tongue lingering on mine. The kiss left me unsatisfied, yearning for more. A lot more.

I finish drying myself, brush the hair out of my face, and slide some clean boxers over my junk. Grabbing it firmly to rearrange it, so we're both good to go. My mind is getting cloudy as my hunger is growing. It's now or never. With Miles being out, the time to finally put an end to this series of fortunate events has come.

And God knows I like to win! I grin to myself, pulling up my grey joggers.

Back to the living room, I sit on the sofa, turn Netflix on and scroll down the menu when Sophie joins me. Her hair still wet, her bare face still looking flustered, she sits at a good distance from me, wrapped up in flowy shorts and an oversized shirt.

"Does movie night sounds good?" I ask. "I also ordered pizza; it should be here shortly."

"Fine by me," she nods, grabbing a cushion in her arms. "Did you have anything particular in mind?"

I shrug and lean forward.

"Oh, I have a few ideas, Princess, but I am still trying to figure out if you'd be interested."

"I am curious now, so you might as well tell me," she replies, grinning, shuffling closer.

I wet my lips as I study her angelic face and tell her, almost whispering: "I really want to continue what you started in the shower."

Her eyes instantly widen, roaming over my body. I grin and feel my cock involuntary twitch while she squeezes the cushion she's holding and subtly pulls it deeper between her thighs.

"Let's start with the pizza, shall we?" she breathes, her voice almost failing her.

"If you insist," I add, smiling even more.

"I'm now wondering if your mouth has any uses other than talking shit, Dalton."

"You said you wanted to start with the pizza, Princess."

She laughs, observing me sideways, obviously imagining, once again, all the ways my mouth could be of use to her.

Just… you… wait, Princess…

After some negotiations, we agree on Howl's Moving Castle, a good choice considering our full attention won't be directed at the screen, as I have other plans in mind.

The doorbell rings, signaling the start of the first round.

"I'll be right back."

I get up to get the pizza and pick up two beers from the kitchen on my way back.

"Meateor or Bangin' BBQ?" I inquire, opening the boxes.

"I beg your pardon?"

"The meaty one or the meatier one?"

"Meateor, please. Luckily, I'm hungry for meat."

I bet you are.

I give her her beer and open mine taking a long sip before grabbing the Bangin' BBQ box.

"Are you going to eat all of it?"

I offer her a carnivorous smile and nod. She shakes her head and starts eating her slice. The movie is entertaining enough, but my attention is wandering elsewhere.

On Sophie's shoulder, to be exact. Her shirt is slowly falling, revealing more skin. No need to guess she's not wearing anything else as I peek at her hardened nipples under the thin layer of cotton.

Turning to me, she whispers: "Do you think Miles will be back at all tonight?"

I glance at her as she is biting her lower lip, devouring me whole with her beautiful watery eyes.

And it's on. Round two.

Tilting my head, my hair drops from my shoulders and covers half of my face.

I'm in character, feeling the dominance I'm now able to assert over her.

"Are you... afraid to be alone with me?"

"You're so full of yourself," she adds, rolling her eyes, not as sassy as before.

I lean in and whisper: "No, I'm not, but I'm wondering how full of me you want to be."

She holds my gaze, her cheeks now looking bright pink, but shakes her head.

"Now, now, Captain, don't get too ahead of yourself, yet," she snorts while pushing me back playfully. "I am happy for him, Charles seems to be a good man."

She's not there yet. Ok!

"He's a decent guy, yeah," I reply. "I've known him a while."

"I remember seeing him a few times," she ponders. "But it's kind of vague."

Her voice trembles, the small talk and the screen are now just a pretext. She's still thinking about whether she can give in or not. I can now feel the relentless tapping of her heel on the floor.

Let's try the oldest trick in the book.

I smile, strategically placing my hand over her shoulder and lightly caress the nape of her neck.

Sophie's now not really watching the screen anymore, she seems interested in something else entirely.

I feel her twitch and fidget beside me.

Some goosebumps form under my touch, and I continue. Her skin is soft, and I enjoy how she reacts to me. She places her hand on my thigh and starts drawing circles on it. Her touch is light, and I appreciate the warmth it creates.

As much as I like our little duel, I want her to make the first move. She already did when we were in the shower, and I know she wants it as much as I do. Now it's on me to bare the wait, and it's getting hard.

Ready when you are Princess…

I hope Netflix isn't asking if we're still watching cause we're not. She turns her face towards me, little flames dancing in her inquisitive eyes. I slowly put pressure on her back with my hand so she moves closer. Time freezes as I take in all of her features.

She wants it. I know she does.

There's no way back now, we will finish what we started. This week. Years ago.

"Are you done eating, Princess? Ready for dessert?" I tease, my face just a few centimeters from hers.

"Why don't you just show m-"

My lips collide with hers before she can finish her sentence. My kiss is hard, violent, and freeing as an electric shock runs through my spine. She moans into my mouth as I slide my hands up her shirt over the contour of her curves before cupping her breasts.

She's soft, hot, and I'm getting so fucking hard for her.

I'll make you scream, call on God and beg for mercy, and I'll make sure you enjoy every second of this!

I pick her up by the hips and sit her on my lap, she wraps her legs around me, looking famished, licking her cherry-red and swollen lips. She entangles her fingers in my hair and tugs at it. She tells me how hard it was to hold back.

I just click my tongue and slowly peel off her shirt, then lean back, taking her in.

"Tell me, Sophie…" I groan, guiding her hips upwards.

"Tell you what?" she replies, practically panting.

"Tell me how long you've been dreaming of this exact moment?"

"Shut up, Dalton!" she whines while I close my mouth on her tit, tasting her skin, tormenting it with my tongue and teeth.

Her grasp on my hair stiffens, and I feel her nails gliding down, one painful way to say she likes it.

Smirking, I explore her neck, her shoulders, and her breasts with my tongue. She tastes of coconut and salt, and her sweet scent of heat makes me crave her cunt. I'm staying silent, in control, yet I'm boiling inside. She shivers and arches her back when I nibble her other breast. Her moans make me tense in anticipation, my chest is heaving, and I growl as her fingers tug even more at my hair.

"Easy, Princess, you wouldn't want to push me now, would you?"

She opens her eyes, a faint smile playing on her lips.

"Are you so eager to punish me, Daddy?" she pouts, tugging at my hair again.

"That was my last warning, Kitten."

The blushing beauty defies me one more time.

"Kitty's got claws," she sassily announces.

Ding ding ding! Round three.

While pinching her reddened nipple a little harder, I start caressing her arm with my fingers. Running them up her wrist, past the fold of her elbow, the curve of her shoulder, and the shape of her collarbone until I very slowly but firmly wrap them around her pretty little throat.

"You leave me no choice, Princess. At least take it like a good girl."

The tip of her tongue slides against her teeth as she nods.

I tighten my grip so close to her face, I can feel her hot breath on me.

"From now on, you are mine, and mine only. You will comply and do as I say WHEN I say it. Do you understand?"

She nods again while I notice one wanderous hand sliding down her chest to attend to the growing urge between her thighs.

"Let's start here, Princess, and then, I'll have you in my bed."

"Are you sure we won't be bothered?" she whispers.

Nodding, I can't help but laugh hearing her. This comment's so innocent and pure.

"I promise we have the whole night to ourselves," I say while caressing her soft, pale skin. "Now, lay on the couch for me."

She leans forward and claims my lips once again, kissing me deeply. I kiss her back but keep the juicy flesh of her lower lip between my teeth, nibbling it hard enough for her to squeal.

I let her go and enunciate: "I said… get on the fucking couch."

Timidly, she obeys and lays down on the sofa, anxiously waiting for my next move.

I gently slide her shorts down and pause, smirking, taking her all in while my hand slides very slowly down her exposed body, tracing lines from her breasts to her inner thighs.

She stares at me with very hungry eyes as I close the space to her quivering pussy. Her scent is sweet, I wish to relish in it, but for now.

From between her legs, my eyes riveted to her, I demand: "Touch yourself."

She raises an eyebrow as I get up and remove my shirt.

"I thought you wanted…"

"What I want, Kitten, is to watch you work your cunt as you did all week thinking about me."

Sophie frowns, unsure, but cautiously moves her fingers down until she reaches her clit. The other hand on her chest, eyes closed, she starts caressing herself, her hips slowly starting to sway along to her rhythm.

"*Open* your eyes," I command. "I want you to look at me."

Her cheeks turn fiery red again, but she opens them and holds my gaze, as requested.

"Good girl!" I smile. "Now spread your legs wider. Show me how hard you want it."

She bites her lips as she lifts up and opens her thighs, gifting me the excruciatingly exciting sight of her dripping wet pussy, rosy, offered, and her swollen clit, as she rolls it relentlessly under her expert fingers. So expert that her short breath and opened mouth are signals enough for me to add more rules to this game.

"Slow down, Princess."

"But…" she quivers.

I shake my head and put my hand over hers.

"Your pleasure is mine, remember? I will decide when you can cum. And now is not the time."

"Oh!"

"Now, hold it a little longer."

She slows down, her face telling me she's now very aroused by our little role-play. Looking at her offering herself up to me makes me even harder than before.

Thank God for joggers.

Hovering over her, I blow lightly on her throbbing clit. She gasps, and moans, and these are the sweetest sounds I've heard in a while. I'm having a really hard time controlling myself.

Her hands tremble as I know she wishes to resume her caress or grab and slam my face on her now needy little cunt.

Sadistically, I lap up her clit once. Twice. She cries for me to eat her up.

"Tut tut tut, who's the master here?"

"You are." she shivers.

"Good girl."

I deeply inhale the scent of her inner thigh and then bite it. She jumps, quivers, and lets out the most exquisite moan as I suck it in enough so she will bear my mark.

I get up to see her panting, aching to end this delicious torture.

"Finger yourself now," I demand.

She smiles, excited and licking her lips mischievously while she slides two fingers inside herself, thrusting them in more with increasing urgency. Approaching the edge.

Her eyes almost revulsed, frowning, she swears, she whines and whimpers uncontrollably. Leaning forward, I place my hand over hers and nibble her ear.

"Not yet, Princess," I groan. "Remember, I decide."

She softly cries, "Fuck me, Dalton!"

I smile against her ear.

"When I get to 1, you'll be free."

She whimpers again as my fingers press against her swollen clit. Breathing hard, my face buried in her neck, I start counting down.

"10… 9…"

I lean back a bit, making sure I can see the pure lust on her exquisite face. My movements are sure, deliberate. She groans as I lick her lips.

"8… 7…"

I remove her fingers and slide three of my own inside of her. Her pussy is hot, drenched, and open as I tease her gspot deeper.

"6… 5…"

Gripping the couch, she silently screams, her mouth forming an O, her eyes open in disbelief as she unexpectedly squirts all over my hands. I grin and slow down again, making sure she is just on the verge of breaking. As I get down on her, lapping her dripping, pulsing clit again and again.

"4… 3…"

The way she looks at me, her face, her supplications, they are even better than what I could've possibly imagined.

"Almost there, baby… 2…"

Almost tearful, she looks at me, pleading for me to let her release. This turns me on so much I could get off right here as I reach the end of the countdown.

"1…"

Under my touch, she shatters. Overwhelmed, the face she offers me is everything I hoped for. Arching her back, her whole body convulses. Sophie moans loudly, my name escaping from her lips several times. Her thighs shaking with spasms of pleasure, her juices flowing on my fingers as I help her surf her orgasm, and nothing compares to the way she looks at me. Teary-eyed, out of breath, an incredulous yet content smile stretching her lips is as satisfactory to me as it is to her.

"Wow!" she sighs, her eyes twinkling, while I bring my fingers to my lips and lick them clean.

That was the appetizer, now, the plat de résistance.

Without adding anything, I offer her my hand to get up and lead her into the hallway to my room. After inviting her in, kicking the door closed behind us, I lean against it, embracing the view of her naked body. Her shoulders, the small of her back, her ass.

Plump, soft, beautiful.

My sweet temptation.

She turns around, playful, a wry half-smile on her lips, ready for an encore, and puts her body on me, her hands exploring my sides, her eyes free-falling into mine.

Or the other way around.

"You've been very good, Princess."

"Thank you, Daddy," she replies, kissing my lips, her nails running down my back, inside my joggers, until she reaches my ass. "Should we take these off?"

"We're a little impatient, aren't we?" I sneer, grabbing her hands, turning her around to pin her against the wall.

She giggles and grinds her sweet ass against my erection.

You little brat!

"What did I say earlier about pushing me, Kitten?"

Turning around to look at me, she suppresses a little sly smile and retorts. "That it will get me in trouble."

I nod, pulling down my sweatpants and boxers, finally freeing my cock. Sophie looks at it and smacks her lips with appetite as her fingers leave my waist. Raising them to her mouth to lick them, her eyes riveted to mine, she asks, "Will THAT get me in trouble?"

Her slippery hand wrapped around my cock, she adds, squeezing a bit harder, "Tell me, Daddy, do you prefer me pushing you? Or pulling?"

I close my eyes and groan as she starts slowly moving up and down. Her hand feels good, her fresh grasp around my hot pulsating skin. I'm allowing her to play a little longer, but I want to feel her fully. I soundly kiss her before facing her against the wall, restraining her wrists above her head. She tries to glance at me, but my grip on her neck is firm as to what my intentions are.

"There, there, be good, behave."

She giggles and complies, a glutton for what's to come.

Looking her over, my fingers leave her neck to trace a line down her spine, soft, gentle, caressing the roundness of her ass cheek before smacking it.

She gasps.

I slap it again. Harder.

She shivers and whines.

I smile.

"Do you like that, Princess?"

She moans, nodding and arching her back even more, offering the plain sight of her ass, starting to redden under my touch.

One or two more slaps get her more aroused than expected as I slide a finger over her sensitive pussy.

She's wet again.

"Don't turn around just yet," I order.

While I get a condom from my dresser, I'm just amazed by how good the chemistry is between us. She's docile yet sassy, she's into our little game more than I'd have expected, and moreover, she trusts me with it.

Damn, this is gonna be good.

Tearing the foil with my teeth as she can't resist eyeing me with greed and envy while I unroll the rubber over my erection. Getting closer to her, tipping her hips towards me, I wrap a hand around her neck.

"What did I say, Kitten?" I ask, kissing her shoulder.

"To not turn around."

She pants.

"That's damn right," I nod, licking her neck until I bite it hard.

She trembles.

"And what did you do?" I ask again, spreading her legs, fondling into her wet entrance.

"I disobeyed."

"You sure did!"

I slide my painfully hard cock inside her, all the way in, as she cries in pleasure.

"Punish me, Daddy!"

Fuck, she's good.

I readjust my grip on her throat as she gasps, tilting her head back, opened mouth, eyes closed. Her nails are already scratching the wall as I hold myself to her mellow hips, thrusting forward. Her cunt's warm and wet, pressing all around me. Pulling her closer, I tell her how hard she's making me, how obedient and beautiful she is, and how sweet she tastes. Growling lowly as I push in and out of her, I spank her again, harder this time.

"Again, Daddy!" she pleads.

I happily oblige a few more times, increasing the sting each time. Sophie's cries and her body tremors as I slam deep into her are driving me mad. She's dripping, sweating, and screaming at me to fuck her harder.

I won't be able to hold on much longer. I swear I'm not done with her, far from it.

"Come for me, Daddy," she whispers as she senses I am close to the edge.

Sliding my hand from her neck to her breast, I squeeze it and bite her shoulder, imprinting my teeth into her porcelain skin, unleashing my pleasure. I groan loudly as I cum. The feeling's amazing.

Panting, I look at her to cup her face between my hands, kissing her deeply.

She smiles when I notice the marks I left on her.

"You didn't joke when you told me I'll be yours, did you?"

"And I still don't! You ARE mine tonight, Sophie. Now be a good girl and go wait for me on the bed."

"What do you have in mind?"

I slap her ass one more time as she obeys and passes me by.

"You'll see…"

She hops on the bed, waiting, as I go to my bathroom, splash water over my face, and smirk thinking about my next move, as I roll around in my hand a black silk scarf.

Walking back to her, I stop, taking her in once again. Sitting on her heels, knees apart, she softly caresses her breast, her thighs, inviting me to join her.

I stop in front of her, showing her the blindfold between my hands.

"Do you trust me?"

"What do you want to do to me?"

"Just a surprise, nothing too extreme."

She touches my forearm, caressing it until she takes the blindfold and applies it over her eyes.

"You're my master, and I am yours."

Her words make me shiver.

Crawling into bed, I slide under her, grabbing her by the hips as I pull her down over my face. She squeals, realizing what's about to happen.

Grinning, I lick her clit slowly.

"Dalton," she whispers.

"Yes, Princess?" I say, letting my tongue caress her again.

"Fucking hell!"

Chuckling, I position myself better, intoxicated by her intimate perfume, relishing in it, my fingers anchoring her ass tightly while I suck, bite, and lick her pussy. Her taste after orgasm is salty yet sweet. She tastes like rain and kiwi fruit. Sophie lets herself go and properly sits on my face. She's wet, shivering, and burning as I enjoy all the emotions she's going through. The noises escaping her mouth are the most obscenely exciting I've heard so far. Who knew she could be so crude?

So exquisitely dirty.

I have her begging again as I insert three fingers inside of her. While she swears, her body leaning forward, I keep her balanced while my tongue works circles around her clit.

Come on, Princess, I can feel you're almost there.

Crooking my fingers, pressing her flesh ruthlessly, I tease her clitoris again, blowing over it. She squeals, trying to escape from the relentless torture, but I keep her body close to me.

"Cum for me again, Princess."

"Make me," she coyly replies.

Oh, it's like that, huh?

Thrusting in her furiously in tune with her gasps and screams, I give everything to her until she finally gives in. Arching her back, she moves her hips uncontrollably as her cunt tightens hard around my fingers, and she cums again, my name and some more insults rolling off of her tongue repeatedly. I slide back laughing while Sophie falls on the sheets panting before removing the blindfold.

Looking at me, she smiles, seeing my very satisfied expression at first and then my erection.

The whole face-sitting experience got me rock-hard and wanting for more. Again.

Sophie bats her lashes, gets on her knees, and asks, shyly: "May I suck your dick, please, Daddy?"

Feeling my cock twitch, I ponder for a moment. I was clearly not done with her, but I could let her have a little bit of fun. Leaning, I pull up her chin and suck on her lips.

I simply nod.

The smile she gives me puts fire from my heart to my balls. The ways she has to get to me are beyond my understanding. She's good. She's who I want, who I need.

Still smiling voraciously as I lean back on the bed, she kneels before my swollen cock, licking it from the base to the tip, her defiant eyes darting to mine. I groan and surrender for once, letting my head fall back as the warmth of her mouth closes around my shaft. Sophie moves up and down, twirling her tongue and teasingly scratching me with her teeth. I get even harder when she takes me deeper into her throat.

"Princess," I growl, grabbing her hair. "That's enough."

It costs me to stop her, but she gave me the power tonight, and I intend to use it as much as she knows how to work her beautiful mouth.

I pull her up and ask her again to stop. She pouts but complies, not before licking me whole one last time.

"You've been a good girl; you've got me all hard. Do you know what I'm going to do to you now?"

She looks at me with doe eyes and shakes her head. I smirk, stretch, grab another condom from the nightstand, and sheath it onto my shaft. Leaning, I catch her and kiss her deeply, pulling her onto my lap. Sophie's still shaky and sticky from her previous orgasms. I love the scent of sex on her, the sweet, the sour, the smell of corruption, and the taste of lust that lingers on both of us. I observe her, the fire still dancing in her eyes, the inextinguible thirst, I bury my face in her skin, kissing every available part of her body. Grinding against me, pulling my hair, so she faces me better, and finds my lips again, moaning as she kisses me, her tongue caressing mine. I can still taste her flavor mixed with mine, and it drives me mad.

I groan and pick her up, sliding her all the way down my erection. She's burning from the inside, and I feel her melting around me. Soft. Hot. Liquid.

Leaning in, I suck on her nipple, hardening it to the point of pain. She gasps as my fingers grip her hips, and I bite her. I am torn between being rough or gentle with her.

"I don't plan on being gentle right now. Are you okay with that?"

"You are in charge," she whispers.

"Say that again. I'm gonna fuck you hard, Sophie."

"I want you to fuck me hard, Daddy."

"Good girl."

I move her forcefully up and down, her body offered up to me. Grunting, I wrap my hand around her neck and lean close to her.

"Are you going to cum again for me, Sophie?"

Her eyes on mine, she nods, flashes a wide smile, and slides a hand down her stomach before her fingers reach her clit.

"As you wish, Master."

Her words are like fire on gasoline. Hotter than anything. I can't believe how willing and obedient she is. Thinking about it arouses me even more. Her red flesh between my fingers, I bite and mark her again. She moans and cries, louder and louder, her body following the rhythm I impose. Sophie caresses her clit frantically, and I feel her cunt starting to clench around my cock.

"Not yet, Kitten."

I slow down and fondle her breast, pinching her nipple until she whines and begs.

"Oh my, fuck! Daddy, I can't! Let me cum!"

"Beg me, Kitten."

"Please, Daddy, please!"

Sophie's pleading look will be the death of me. As painful as it is, I need to slow down.

"Do you deserve to cum? Have you been good enough, Princess?"

She whines and nods, biting her lower lip, tears shining in the corners of her eyes, her fingers still circling her clit. I push a strand of hair away from her face and start thrusting in and out of her again. She clenches around my cock again, and I slow down, loving this delicious torture.

"Alright, Kitten, it's time."

I pound into her, my eyes on her as she melts into my arms once more. Arching her back, Sophie undulates, her nails digging into my flesh. She screams her pleasure as she crumbles.

"DALTON! FUCKING HELL!"

I flip her over on the bed and slide my cock back into her wet cunt. All Hell breaks loose as I ram deeply into her core. Sophie, still sensitive, cries for mercy, but I keep pushing deeper and deeper. My hand on her throat, I squeeze tighter and bite and lick her shoulder. Plunging into her a few more times, I groan, releasing my load. Her name escapes my lips a few times while my orgasm hits me. A wave of molten lava, bliss, and oblivion.

Out of breath and out of mind, I roll onto my back as she turns to me. I pull her closer, kissing the marks I left on her skin.

"Are you okay, Princess?"

She lifts her head towards me and smiles, offering me a blissful, content expression. Her cheeks are cherry red, and her eyes sparkling, like she went on the best Ferris wheel. I chuckle, caressing her arm.

That was a hell of a ride, indeed.

After a few minutes of silence, Sophie gets up from the bed. I frown, looking at her.

"Where are you going?"

"Bathroom and then back to my room, I guess."

I shake my head firmly.

"You're coming back here after, there's no way you'll be sleeping in your bed tonight."

She shyly smiles.

"Your wish is my command."

Careful what I could wish for.

***

Sophie left with Miles early this morning, leaving me feeling kinda bittersweet. The night was short, but it was worth every second. I was able to steal a few moments with her before her departure, and finding myself looking forward to our next encounter is a bit unexpected on my part.

Though I'm pretty sure, I've made quite an impression on her, and vice versa, I don't know if or when this will happen again.

Filling my cup with hot fresh coffee, I let my eyes wander around and fall upon a yellow square of paper and hideous butterflies.

My cell phone shines and has me smirking.

SOPHIE

[Hope you liked your week Daddy.]

DALTON

[It was okay Princess. ;)]

SOPHIE

[You weren't bad yourself.]

DALTON

[Show a little respect, will you?]

SOPHIE

[Fine Master. I promise to be better next time.]

DALTON

[That's my good girl.]

About the Author

Fiery redhead from Montreal, guardian of French (Canadian) language, and defender of honest camaraderie. M. S. Spencer is known for her love of words, music, and long-haired and mysterious Adonises, apparently so, among other things.

Writing Sweet Temptation is the achievement of what was merely a bet for her. A wish. A dream. Yet, here she is, forever flabbergasted and grateful.

Instagram: ms_spencer_author

TikTok: ms_spencer_author

Printed in Great Britain
by Amazon